In memory of Dan Mooney—dear friend,
fine pianist, and great teacher

Library of Congress Cataloging-in-Publication Data

Parker, Robert Andrew.

Piano starts here: the young Art Tatum/

Robert Andrew Parker.—1st ed.   p. cm.

ISBN 978-0-375-83965-8 (alk. paper)

ISBN 978-0-375-93965-5 (lib. bdg.)

1. Tatum, Art, 1910–1956—Childhood and youth—Juvenile literature.

2. Jazz musicians—United States—Biography—Juvenile literature. I. Title.

ML3930.T2P37 2008

786.2'165092—dc22

[B] 2006102105

The text of this book is set in Archetype.

The illustrations are rendered in watercolor.

PRINTED IN CHINA

1 3 5 7 9 10 8 6 4 2

First Edition

PIANO STARTS HERE

THE YOUNG ART TATUM BY ROBERT ANDREW PARKER

schwartz & wade books · new york

This is the house in Toledo where I was born.

This is my father.

He's a mechanic.

This is my mother. She often sings in the church down the street, but she isn't singing here. She has too much cleaning to do.

This is the living room. That's the piano. Every once in a while my mother plays it,
but otherwise it sits quietly in the corner.

One day, I can reach the keyboard on tiptoe. I play with one finger, then two fingers, then my fists and hands.

My mother says, "That sounds nice, do that again," and I do, until she says, "Enough now. Why don't you go play while it's still light outside?"

But because of my bad eyes, day and night, dark and light, don't really matter to me. Not the way sounds and smells do—piano notes, streetcar bells, corn bread baking in the oven.

As I get older, my eyesight gets worse. An operation helps—but just a little.

Still, bad eyes can't keep me from playing the piano. My hands get to know the keys, the short black ones on top and long white ones below. I play more and more. And more.

When my father leaves in the morning now, he gives me a quick hug and says, "Don't wear out that piano today." In the evening when my mother calls me to supper, I say, "I'll be right back, Piano, don't go away."

Just after my tenth birthday, Reverend Johnson asks me to play in church. I love our church—the way it smells like soap, furniture polish, and flowers; the way footstep sounds echo off the walls. Still, I feel nervous.

But when I touch the keys, all my fear vanishes. My foot taps the rhythm, and my notes fill the space between the music of everyone's voices.

Afterward, Martha Chemples asks me to play at the annual YMCA bake sale. Mrs. Bradford asks if I can play at Mr. Bradford's seventieth birthday party. My mother says, "He can't be out late," but she squeezes my shoulder, and I know she is pleased.

On summer evenings when it is too hot to even turn on the lights, my parents sit on the porch swing with my little brother and sister. The neighborhood children run around catching lightning bugs in mayonnaise jars.

As their jars grow brighter, they hear my music pouring out our window. I play "Moonlight Bay" and "Shine On, Harvest Moon"—all the moon songs I can think of. "My, my, isn't he something," my mother says into the night.

Denise and Janet, twin sisters who live next door, walk me to school every day now. They make sure I don't get lost or step in front of a streetcar.

In class, Denise sits next to me and helps me. And on assembly days, the principal, Mrs. Hendricks, asks me to play.

My father never says much about my music, but I know he's listening. Sometimes he even dances. Though he hardly moves, I can feel his big feet shake the floor. His rhythm matches mine, and I imagine I'm playing with a bass player tap-tapping his feet and slap-slapping his fingers. When I start "Memphis Blues," my father pulls my mother from the kitchen, throws her apron on a chair, and swings her across the floor until she laughs in spite of herself.

After school I spend a lot of time at the Pick-a-Rib café around the corner. Mr. Bartlett, the owner, is a friend of my father's, and he lets me use his player piano. I like to wind up the handle and hear the keys move by themselves. Then I play.

Sometimes Mr. Bartlett comes out of the kitchen and says, "Arthur, was that you or the piano?" And other times he says, "Well, I know that was you—the player piano isn't that fast!"

One night my father and his friend Eddie take me to a bar nearby. My father finds me a chair and whispers, "Play 'Tiger Rag' just like you heard it on the radio, only faster." And because it is so noisy and smoky and crowded, I'm not nervous.

As soon as my notes fill the air, the whole place grows still. Everyone at the bar stops drinking, people at tables stop eating. Waitresses stop serving.

When I play a song I heard on the radio, an old man starts to clap along. Couples start dancing. They buy drinks for my father and Eddie, and a ginger ale for me, stuffing coins in my pockets till I'm sure the money'll spill onto the floor.

I play all the tunes I know. The bartender, whistling a few bars of a song, asks, "Do you know that one?" I put my hands on the keyboard and say, "You mean this one?" and play some more.

When I begin "Humoresque," the room becomes quiet. I imagine I am in a boat on a lake, the moon shining through the trees, and I feel sad. I wonder, does music float up through the ceiling and through the roof and then up through the sky? Do the sounds keep going until they reach the stars?

We get home very late and don't wake my mother. In the morning I go to school and my father goes to work, as if nothing has changed.

That afternoon, I take my coins and buy my mother a round gold music box. When I lift the lid, a tiny tinkle comes out that sounds like a mouse playing "Whispering." I buy my father a baseball mitt to put in his lunch pail so he can play catch during his break at the factory.

Almost every night, my father and Eddie walk me to local
bars or we ride the streetcar to ones far away. Sometimes my
name is on a sign outside and people come just to hear me.
Now when I play, my fingers do everything I want them to.
I can make them whistle, I can make them sing. I can play one
song and then weave another song in and out and through it.

I often hide a song inside another and another—"After
You've Gone" inside "Poor Butterfly," and almost always a
few bars of "Humoresque" inside them both.

One day, Mr. Storer asks me to play at his radio station,
five days a week, for more money than I have ever imagined.

Once people start hearing me on the radio, I'm asked to play all over the country. My music takes me farther and farther from home.

When I am at the piano, I close my eyes. I play clouds of notes, rivers of notes, notes that sound like skylarks singing and leaves rustling, like rain on a rooftop. I forget that my eyes aren't good. I have everything I need.

Bandleaders call me. I tour with musicians through Ohio, to Chicago, Kansas City, and even New York City. I play with Adelaide Hall, Slam Stewart, and Tiny Grimes. I become famous.

But still, late at night, as people sway around me and my foot is tapping, I think of our house in Toledo, of my mother and father and sister and brother. I think of Reverend Johnson, Eddie, and the twins. No matter where I am, when the room fills with my music, I remember all the people who helped me. The people I love.

ART TATUM AND ME

In 1946 I went to 52nd Street in New York City, where most of the jazz greats played—and I heard Lester Young, Ben Webster, Roy Eldridge, Beryl Booker, and Art Tatum. Tatum was on piano, with Tiny Grimes on guitar and Slam Stewart on bass. The place was jammed, and Tatum was amazing. He was very heavy then, and he had a lopsided smile; after a particularly dazzling run on the piano keys he would glance up, grinning, as if to say, "How about that?"

That night Tatum was thirty-six years old and had already been playing professionally for more than twenty years. I was nineteen and still in the army. Since then I've spent a lot of my time listening to Tatum's music and reading about his life. Most books about Tatum follow his adult years, but I've always been curious about his early ones. In this book, I used whatever details of Tatum's childhood I could find, along with my imagination, to fill in the missing pieces.

MORE ABOUT ART TATUM

Art Tatum, the oldest of three children (a fourth died in infancy), was born in Toledo, Ohio, on October 13, 1910. He was born with severely limited vision, which worsened as he grew older. He had numerous operations to improve his sight, but none of them was very successful.

Growing up, Tatum learned music from every source he could find—phonograph records and player pianos, local musicians and the radio. He had some formal training. He practiced constantly, and by 1926, he was playing professionally around Toledo.

As an adult, Tatum toured with the Speed Webb Band. He also performed with a popular singer, Adelaide Hall, with whom he made his first recording in 1932. Art heard and was heard by all the great jazz pianists of the time—musicians like Teddy Wilson, Earl Hines, Fats Waller. They were amazed by both his improvisational brilliance and his incredible technique. Classical players, too, were awed. In 1938 Tatum played in London, to enthusiastic crowds. In Paris that same year, he performed in orchestra halls and sat in as a guest pianist with local musicians at nightclubs, bistros, and wherever else jazz was played.

Tatum would effortlessly incorporate into his music bits of popular songs like "Camptown Races," "The Stars and Stripes Forever," and "Danny Boy." But by far his favorite piece to include was a humoresque by Czech composer Antonín Dvořák.

Life for Tatum in the late 1930s was a busy routine of club dates, recording sessions, and endless traveling. There were long bus rides, bad food, card games, shooting pool, and too much drinking. His health suffered, and diabetes became a problem. Still, he remained jolly. He was very generous, made friends easily, and was hailed as an incomparable pianist everywhere he went. When he entered a club or a bar, it wasn't uncommon for someone to say, "God is in the room." Other pianists were often too intimidated to play in his presence.

In 1947 Tatum started touring with music producer Norman Granz, whose concerts were called "Jazz at the Philharmonic" and featured the greatest jazz musicians available.

These well-organized concerts played in major cities around the United States. In 1953 Granz convinced Tatum to record, and the result was a series of fourteen brilliant albums. Eventually Tatum's poor health worsened. He died on November 5, 1956, at the age of forty-six.

In the world of jazz, there have been a few giants whose talents will probably never be surpassed: Louis Armstrong, Benny Goodman, Buddy Rich, Charlie Parker, Duke Ellington, and—of course—Art Tatum.

BIBLIOGRAPHY

Balliett, Whitney. *Collected Works: A Journal of Jazz, 1954–2001*. New York: St. Martin's Press, 2000.

Collier, James Lincoln. *The Making of Jazz: A Comprehensive History*. New York: Houghton Mifflin, 1978.

Crow, Bill. *From Birdland to Broadway: Scenes from a Jazz Life*. New York: Oxford University Press, 1992.

Giddins, Gary. *Riding on a Blue Note*. New York: Oxford University Press, 1981.

Hodeir, André. *Jazz, Its Evolution and Essence*. New York: Grove Press, 1956.

Horricks, Raymond, et al. *These Jazzmen of Our Time*. London: Victor Gollancz, 1960.

Lester, James. *Too Marvelous for Words: The Life and Genius of Art Tatum*. New York: Oxford University Press, 1994.

Schuller, Gunther. *The Swing Era: The Development of Jazz, 1930–1945*. New York: Oxford University Press, 1989.